# Fun with the Moles

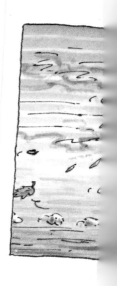

# Fun with the
# Molesons

Stories by **Burny Bos**

Illustrated by **Hans de Beer**

*Translated by J. Alison James*

**North-South Books**
New York / London

Copyright © 2000 by Nord-Süd Verlag AG, Gossau Zürich, Switzerland
First published in Switzerland under the title *Familie Maulwurf Dicke Luft!*
English translation copyright © 2000 by North-South Books Inc.

First published in the United States, Great Britain, Canada,
Australia, and New Zealand in 2000 by North-South Books,
an imprint of Nord-Süd Verlag AG, Gossau Zürich, Switzerland.

Distributed in the United States by North-South Books Inc., New York.

Library of Congress Cataloging-in-Publication Data is available.
A CIP catalogue record for this book is available from The British Library.
ISBN 0-7358-1353-1 (trade binding)
1  3  5  7  9  TB  10  8  6  4  2
ISBN 0-7358-1354-X (library binding)
1  3  5  7  9  LB  10  8  6  4  2
Printed in Belgium

For more information about our books, and the authors and artists
who create them, visit our web site: www.northsouth.com

# Contents

# Meet the Molesons

If you don't know my family already, you're not in for any big surprises.

We are pretty ordinary. My mother's name is Molly, that's her with the hose. She works in an office, which is pretty boring. My father has more fun, because he takes care of things around the house, like my sister and me. His name is Morris. Dusty, my twin sister, and I go to school, of course. And then there is our grandma, who always has a trick up her sleeve. My name is Dug, short for Dugless. That's me with the red hat and my eyes closed.

## Musical Beds

Late one night I woke up. Everyone else was asleep. I was cold. I was scared. I think I had a bad dream. I climbed out of bed and tiptoed down the hall to my parents' room. "Mother?" I hissed. "I can't sleep."

"What is it, sweetie?" Mother asked.

"Can I come into your bed?"

"All right," she mumbled.

Happily I crawled in between my parents and went right to sleep.

But back in my room, Dusty woke up. When she saw that I wasn't there, she climbed out of bed and headed right to my parents' room.

She saw me snoozing there and didn't even ask. She just crawled in next to me. For a moment or two, everyone was asleep.

Then Father woke up because he had no covers. "Harumph," he grunted, and sleepily wandered down the hall to my bed. Pretty soon everyone was asleep again.

But not for long. Mother rolled over and almost fell out of bed. She sat up and said, "What are you two doing in here?" But we were both sound asleep, sprawled out across the bed. "I'll just go and sleep by myself," she said, and she went down the hall to our room. She threw back the covers, and plopped down on my bed— right on top of Father.

"Help!" Mother shrieked from surprise.

"Ooof ow!" Father cried.

Their yelling woke up Dusty and me again. We all met in the hall.

"You two—to bed," Father said, holding his belly.

"Which bed?" Dusty asked.

"Your own bed," Mother said. She sounded a little grumpy.

In a few minutes, all of us were fast asleep again. We slept right through breakfast the next day. It was a good thing it was Sunday!

# The Rotten Egg

It was so hot. Dusty called it "roasting cats and dogs." The sweat ran so fast down Mother and Father, they had to mop it up with a bath towel.

"Can we go swimming?" Dusty begged.

"Yes!" I cried. "Let's go to the beach!"

But Mother said, "No. We'll melt in the car on the way there. It's too long a drive, and there will be too many people."

She had a point.

Then Father had an idea. "I know a secret little pond. I've never seen anyone there, and it's only a few minutes away."

At the pond, Father was the first one out of the car. He ran whooping like Tarzan straight for the water.

"Wait for us!" Dusty cried.

"Last one in is a rotten egg!" shouted Father, and in he jumped. But the water didn't even splash. It was muck, and he was stuck.

"Help! I'm sinking in slime!"

Dusty shouted, "Mother, come quick! Father is drowning!"

Mother came running. "What are you doing, Morris?"

"I'm stuck in the mud! Now give me a hand, would you?"

Mother reached for Father's hand. She reached again. But Father was too far out. Dusty and I just closed our eyes. We didn't want to watch our father die being sucked into a cesspool.

Mother ran to the car and got a rope
from the back. She threw Father one end
and cried, "Tie it on tight."

Father knotted it around his belly.

Mother tied the other end on the car.
Then she started the engine.

"Slowly, Mother," cried Dusty.

"I hope the rope holds," I said.

Carefully Mother pulled Father from
the stinking mud. "Get in, children.
We're going home," Mother said.

"But, Mother! We wanted to go
swimming!"

"You can't swim in this muck," Mother
said. "Now we know why no one ever
swam in your father's secret pond."

Father reached to open the door.

"You're not getting in this car," Mother shouted through the closed window. "You smell awful—just like a rotten egg!" So Father had to sit outside in the back of the car like a piece of oversized luggage!

Back at home, Grandma said, "What's that smell?"

"Father didn't look before he leaped," said Dusty.

"He was the first one in, not the last, but he's still a rotten egg," I added.

## Lost and Found

It was a bright and sunny day. We decided to go to the amusement park. Unfortunately just about everybody else had the same idea.

But Mother had come prepared. "The last thing we want," she said, "is for one of us to get lost. So I brought you these nice red caps. Then we will stand out in the crowd."

She forgot that Father hates to stand

out. "I never get lost," he complained.

Mother glared at him, so he put on his hat. But he was so embarrassed, he scuffed his feet. He was sure people were staring at him. He didn't even look at the cool rides. We kept on walking. We never noticed when Father got robbed.

A teenager ran past him and shouted, "Hey, Gramps, can I borrow that sharp-looking cap?"

Before he knew it, the boy snatched
the cap right off Father's head and took
off running.

"Hey, wait a second!" Father cried,
"Give me my cap back!" He chased after
the boy. "My cap! He stole my cap!"

That was about when Mother looked
around. "Where's your father?" she
asked us.

We couldn't see him anywhere. He was off on the other side of the park trying to catch a thief. But how were we to know that?

Mother was annoyed. "He's taken off his cap," she said, shaking her head. "I just know it."

Dusty and I looked at each other. Now we'd have to spend the whole day searching for Father. We were ready to start whining, when Mother surprised us.

"Well," she said, "there's nothing to be done. Let's go on the Ferris wheel."

Dusty must have felt as guilty as I did, because she said, "Let's find Father first. He loves the Ferris wheel."

"Yeah, if we all look, we'll find him in no time," I offered.

Mother seemed surprised. "If you really want to," she said.

It didn't take 'no time.' In fact, it took an hour. We finally found Father in the baby-sitting area. He was sitting on a little chair and staring into space.

"Somebody stole my cap," whimpered Father. He looked very upset.

"It doesn't matter," I said. "You can have my cap. I'll be sure to stay close to you." And that is how I got to be the only one in my family who rode the Ferris wheel without a silly red cap on my head.

## Fit as a Fiddle

One day Dusty and I came home all
excited from school. We had fitness
training for the first time. "Guess what!"
I shouted when I came in the house.

Dusty said, "Today we got to . . ."

"Wait, slow down," Father said, and
smiled. "How about if you take turns
telling me. Otherwise I won't understand
a word."

So we explained slowly and carefully
that we'd started fitness training at
school. "I can do a real sit-up," said
Dusty.

"That's good," said Father. "Fitness keeps you fit. When I was your age, I was fit as a fiddle, tuned to a T. Just take a look at this. . . ."

He lay down on his belly and pushed himself up with his arms. "Can either of you do push-ups?" he asked, puffing.

"Of course, Father," said Dusty, and she did a few. I was on the slippery part of the floor, so it was harder for me to push all the way up.

It was fun to do our exercises in the living room. Father knew another one for us to try. "The bridge," he said. "But be careful. It is a tricky one, very difficult!"

He lay down on his back and put his hands behind his head. Then he pushed his belly up and very slowly walked his hands closer and closer to his feet. Pretty soon, he was bent double, just like a bridge.

We both lay down to try it. But it was hard to figure out where to put our hands. "Father, help us," we said.

But all Father said was, "Oooh! Aaah! Ooow!"

We sat up quickly. Father groaned. "I . . . can't . . . get . . . up!" He started to cry.

What were we supposed to do? We wiped his eyes and wiped his nose until Mother showed up. Fortunately, that was soon.

Shaking her head, Mother looked at Father's wonderful bridge. "What have you done to yourself?" she asked.

"Take me to the doctor!" Father said.

"I should think so," said Mother. "But how can we get you there?"

Then she had an idea.

"Get the ironing board," Mother said to me. She slid it under Father. "Now, Dusty, you get the wheelbarrow."

Dusty, Mother, and I lifted Father on the ironing board up on the wheelbarrow. Then we balanced it while Mother pushed all the way to the doctor's.

By the park, we ran into Grandma. "For heaven's sake!" Grandma cried.

"Don't worry," Mother said. "It's nothing serious."

"Nothing serious?" Father groaned.

"We'll have you fixed up in no time," said the doctor. "One little injection and you will be fit as a fiddle."

"See, Father," Dusty said. "Fitness keeps you fit."

"Yes, it does," I chimed in. "We ought to try it more often."

Father had to laugh.

## Catching a Flick

Father and Mother went out with some friends. Dusty and I were going to stay home with Grandma. But Grandma wanted to do something special. So she buzzed up in her electric wheelchair and said, "Hey, you two! How about we catch a flick?"

"What?" we both asked.

"Let's go to the movies," Grandma explained.

"Wow!" I said.

Dusty gave Grandma a huge kiss.

"Well, hop on and hold on," Grandma

said. And she roared off down the road.

The ticket office had no trouble with wheelchairs. They were happy to sell Grandma three tickets. But when she got inside, there were stairs.

The man inside said, "I'm sorry ma'am, you won't be able to get up the stairs in your wheelchair."

"Poppycock!" blazed Grandma. "Look here, young man. I have purchased three tickets. And I want to see this movie with my grandchildren."

The man shrugged his shoulders. "Sorry," he said.

Dusty and I looked at each other sadly and turned to go.

"Sorry?" Grandma was still there, and she was turning red. "All you can say is sorry? Get your sorry self over here and help me up these stairs!"

The man yelped, "Yes ma'am!" and ran to get help.

Then he and the owner and the ticket
lady and the man from the snack bar each
took a corner of Grandma's wheelchair
and carried her right up the steps.

"Thank you kindly," Grandma said at
the top. "Now you can advertise as
'wheelchair accessible.'"

In the movie, Dusty and I sat on
Grandma's lap. It was higher up.

"You two belong in bed," Mother said. She wasn't even embarrassed.

"We forgot to do our homework," Dusty said.

"For school," I added.

"What kind of homework?" asked Father.

"Autumn collection," Dusty said.

"What on earth is that?" asked Father.

Mother explained it to him.

"Oh," he said. "So you need dry leaves and mushrooms."

"Exactly!" we cried.

"Fine, then," said Mother. "Go to bed. Your father and I will take a walk and get

you some dry leaves. But next time don't leave it for the last minute!"

Father got a shoe box. Mother laid in all the leaves and pine cones and acorns they'd found.

"All we need is a mushroom," said Father.

"Forget the mushroom," said Mother.

"Wait, I've got an idea." Father went to the refrigerator. He found a little tub with mushrooms in it.

"Wonderful idea," said Mother. "The Autumn Collection looks perfect now." Father nodded proudly.

The next morning Father showed us what all the things were in the box and made sure we could tell the difference between the oak, maple, and ash leaves.

At school the teacher thought the display was lovely. That is, until she saw the mushroom.

"I strictly told you not to collect mushrooms!" she said angrily. "Some mushrooms are deadly poisonous."

"But we didn't collect it," I said.

"Our father found it in the refrigerator," Dusty said.

"Growing there?" asked the teacher, her eyebrows raised.

We both laughed. "It could be," Dusty said, "but he said it was a salad mushroom."

"Oh," the teacher said, and then she started to laugh. She laughed until tears ran down her face. "That is too much," she said. "Your homework is just perfect."

"So are our parents," Dusty whispered to me.

# Such an Ordinary Family

These are just a few stories about our family—nothing that any family wouldn't do. I'm sure your family is just as normal as mine. Maybe even just a bit more normal?

# About the Author

**Burny Bos** was born in Haarlem, in the Netherlands. He began his career as a teacher, and in 1973 he started developing children's shows for Dutch radio. Within a few years he was working for Dutch television as well. He has won many prizes for his children's broadcasts, films, and recordings. He has also written over two dozen children's books, including the earlier adventures of the Molesons: *Meet the Molesons*, *More from the Molesons*, and *Leave It to the Molesons!*

# About the Illustrator

**Hans de Beer** was born in Muiden, a small town near Amsterdam, in the Netherlands. He began to draw when he went to school, mostly when the lessons got too boring. He studied illustration at the Rietveld Academy of Art in Amsterdam.

Hans de Beer is the author and illustrator of the popular series of picture books featuring Lars, the Little Polar Bear, which have been published in eighteen languages around the world. He has illustrated many other books, including the first three books about the Molesons.